ANTELOPE

THE
HAUNTING
OF
JOEY M'BASA
by
Rosemary Harris

Illustrated by Bethan Matthews

HAMISH HAMILTON
LONDON

HAMISH HAMILTON LTD

Published by the Penguin Group
Penguin Books Ltd, 27 Wrights Lane, London W8 5TZ, England
Penguin Books USA Inc., 375 Hudson Street, New York, New York 10014, USA
Penguin Books Australia Ltd, Ringwood, Victoria, Australia
Penguin Books Canada Ltd, 10 Alcorn Avenue, Toronto, Ontario, Canada M4V 3B2
Penguin Books (NZ) Ltd, 182–190 Wairau Road, Auckland 10, New Zealand

Penguin Books Ltd, Registered Offices: Harmondsworth, Middlesex, England

First published in Great Britain by Hamish Hamilton Ltd 1996

Text copyright © 1996 by Rosemary Harris
Illustrations copyright © 1996 by Bethan Matthews

1 3 5 7 9 10 8 6 4 2

British Library Cataloguing in Publication Data
CIP data for this book is available from the British Library

ISBN 0-241-13618-0

Set in 15pt Baskerville
Printed in Great Britain by Butler and Tanner Ltd
Frome, Somerset

Chapter One

IT WAS THE day they took us to the Tower of London these things happened. By 'they' I mean Miss Maisie Engleford who teaches history, and Dwight Humdinger who was on a visiting lectureship and stopped by at our school to talk about the American Civil War. As though I hadn't enough to worry me already – history being my worst-ever subject. I have this scientific brain.

Well, the next thing we knew, Miss Engleford was rabbitting on about Richard the Third and the little Princes in the Tower, while Dwight

held her hand behind her desk –
which they thought we couldn't see.
And the *next* next thing, we were all
booked together on a coach to show
Dwight that gloomy old Tower, which
I'd seen twice already.

Luckily, my friend Joey M'basa was
coming too. He's the sort of person
who doesn't let most things bother
him, they flow over his head. I asked
him once what he thought about when
he gets rowed in class, which is often,
and he gave this great thoughtful
smile of his and said, "Harlem
Globetrotters." You can see why he
drives Maisie Engleford mad.

"What's it like, this Tower?" he
asked me, as we were getting on the
coach.

"A pain," I said glumly. "The grizly
bits aren't bad, though the whole
thing's a rip-off really."

"The jewelwy's bwill," said my sister Amaryllis, turning round to give Joey the full treatment – wadiant smile. He winced.

"And there's ghosts evwy square yard," continued Rilly.

"Tell her to pull the other one," I said crisply. "She's only teasing you."

Funny thing about Joey: he's brave as a lion on the football field and

nothing any teacher says causes a
dent. Mention ghosts though, and –
wow! He starts to shake. Swears he's a
"sensitive", whatever that may mean.
Well, actually it means he saw his
Auntie Zeta six months after her
funeral. He was bouncing on the spare
room bed where she used to sleep, and
she burst through the closed door
screeching, "Stop that or I belt you

one, Joey M'basa!" just as she used to in real life. He's never gone near that room since.

"Amaryllis," I said grittily, "the Tower ghosts are just a tourist scam."

Joey looked relieved. He fished a tennis ball out of his pocket. "Will there be any useful walls, Mike?" he asked me. He always has these good games ideas, has Joey.

"Plenty," I told him. The thought cheered us both up no end.

Chapter Two

TOWER HILL WAS crammed with
coaches and hundreds of people
yakking in foreign languages, all
clutching their camcorders. It beats
me why anyone comes thousands of
miles to look at someone else's grotty
old Tower full of things you wouldn't
buy in Portobello Road. It might not
have been a bad sort of place when
there was nothing but seagulls, or
people wielding axes. It would have
surprised them when they were
holding up someone's head if they
could have seen the old place now: us
trudging dismally towards it, Dwight

and Engleford ahead, and tourists
clicking away like geiger counters.

It was sweltering hot. One of the
girls called Elsie Neem-Todd said,
"Please, Miss, I feel sick." She always
does on these outings, I can't see why
her mum still makes her come. Miss
Engleford said, "Oh, for goodness
sake, Elsie!" and led her to a litter bin.
A Yeoman glared at us, which made

me feel hot round the neck. I edged away with Joey. The back of a group is the best place to be on these occasions.

Ahead of us Maisie Engleford was impressing Dwight and the tourists with bits of info. "Then the Princess Elizabeth sat down on the steps before Traitor's Gate and refused to go inside –"

"Jolly sensible. She thought it was overpriced too," I muttered, and got a Look across everybody's head. We fell farther back, to be on the safe side.

We managed to stay that way most of the time. The tour seemed no better third time round, except the gruesome bits. Joey perked up a bit at those – though they were nothing to *Excavator 2* that was showing at our cinema.

When we reached the Bloody Tower

I tried to liven things up by telling Joey, "That's where the two little Princes were murdered by their wicked uncle."

He looked faintly interested. "Why did he do that? Who was he, anyway?"

"*Not* one of the Harlem Globetrotters. He was –"

"Wichard the Third," chimed in Rilly bossily. "He had a humpy shoulder and his howwid enemies called him Wichard Cwookback. People said he killed the Princes because he wanted the Thwone. His little nephew Pwince Edward was going to be king, and *his* little bwother Pwince Wichard was next in line, but when Wichard got wid of them he took the Thwone for himself."

I shot Rilly a dagger look for stealing my thunder. "He had them smothered," I said quickly, claiming the meaty bit. "That's what people said, anyway. They vanished."

"Maisie says it pwobably wasn't Wichard at *all*," said Rilly. "It was King Henwy the Seventh, who slew poor old Cwookback at the battle of Bosworth Field. Henwy wanted the Thwone too, so then he mawwied the little Pwinces' sister and got it that way."

Joey was looking impressed by Rilly's grasp of history.

"I wouldn't marry anyone's sister, not even for a throne," I said crossly. "Anyway, I bet Richard did it."

"And *I* bet their ghosts are pwetty mad about it," said Rilly, teasingly. "Never mind, Joey. I'll hold your hand."

He was looking wobbly again.

"No self-respecting ghosts would hang about here with all these tourists," I said firmly.

What seemed hours later our Maisie was still fluting away, and Dwight responding with "That's really sumpin', kid" at intervals. He had an arm round her waist as they peered into a glass case. The other kids were milling about as bored as I was, and Rilly was looking soulfully at some relic.

"Come on, Joey," I hissed, grabbing him by the arm.

A flood of tourists was coming in like high tide. We slithered between them and pretty soon found ourselves outside on the Green. Near the great central tower a small crowd had gathered round some cameramen. Large bright lights added to the sunshine.

"Perhaps they're filming *Excavator 3*," I suggested hopefully.

"Boring old history again, I bet," grumbled Joey, but he followed me across the Green.

He was right – the actors were in historical costume, looking silly and trying not to see the people gaping. We wriggled through to the front for a better view. Two boys were standing to

one side of the actors. I noticed them
because their clothes were different
from the others'. In a moment they
noticed us too. I saw the younger one
pluck at the older boy's sleeve and
murmur something. I felt sure they
were discussing us because they began
whispering together, eyeing us, and
edging closer to Joey.

Beneath the lights a young woman

was lying on the grass, while a girl in jeans arranged her skirts, and another dabbed some cream over her face that gave off an odd fluorescent glow. A bloke in an eyeshade waved away the girl in jeans, saying, "Okay lying there, Duchess? Try a mug shot, Perce."

A camera swung in above the fluorescent face, while the Duchess pouted wadiantly, like Rilly.

"Now Julie," said Eyeshade.

Another girl, bulging out of yards and yards of velvet, kneeled by the Duchess, gingerly clutching an enormous jar.

"Light that jar," commanded Eyeshade. "Final take. Camera!"

Someone snapped a board together. A guy in a dire black wig and mulberry tights stepped forward, grumbling, "Cover her face, mine eyes

dazzle." The girl called Julie dropped a handkerchief over the Duchess's face, heaved up the jar, and murmured, "You too can dazzle all eyes wearing Tower Products 'Moonglow' skin enhancer."

"Great," beamed Eyeshade.

"Dud," said the cameraman. "We lost the Tower."

Eyeshade exploded. I was spellbound, mentally stacking the words for future use. The two boys, who had moved up beside us, collapsed into stifled giggles.

"Was Moonglow that gunge on her face?" asked Joey innocently.

We were so generally glared at that I thought we'd better shift. I took him by the arm again. "Come on – let's find a wall."

A smartish woman was tripping across the Green towards a timbered house. I heard somebody say "There's the Governor's wife", and I steered Joey well away. In the end we found a good place without Beefeaters where we bounced the ball to and fro a bit. After a time someone else caught it. I turned round. The two boys had followed us.

"Here's your ball. Catch," said the older one to Joey, throwing it to him.

"Thanks. Want to join in?" asked Joey.

"Sure, that's why we're here," said the boy. He sounded so cocksure that I immediately bristled.

Joey didn't seem to mind. He's goodnatured. "Okay. I'm Joey, his name's Mike. What's yours?"

"Ned. This is my brother – Dickon."

"Dick on what?"

"It's his name, stupid."

Joey flushed deep plum, like damsons.

"He's not stupid," I said fiercely. "Are you part of that loony advert?"

Beside them we looked a couple of slouches. They were dressed in real fine leather sleeveless jackets and short boots. Their linen shirts were laced. Their hair was good too – very well cut.

Ned laughed. "We've always taken starring roles. Haven't we, Dickon?"

"Don't tease them. We live here,"

said the younger boy. He was thinnish and very pale, and looked rather nice. He edged up beside his brother who put an arm round him, saying, "Dickon mustn't run about too much. He's been ill. I'll play. He can just stand and catch."

"I know – you must be the Governor's kids," I exclaimed. "We saw your mum just now."

Ned looked at me with a sort of

curly superior smile. I felt he was mocking me somewhere inside. "Our father's dead. We're in the Governor's care."

"Poor you, having no dad," said Joey.

Ned shrugged. "We have each other."

I liked him more when he said that. It sounded sincere.

"And we have an uncle," piped up Dickon. "I'm named after him. Uncle Dickie's tough, but he's all right."

"Come on, let's play," I suggested. A breeze had got up – you get them round tall buildings like that Tower. I'd been sweaty and now I felt quite cold. I grabbed the ball from Joey and got it in play, determined to show we were as good as they were.

Joey thought of a good game, a bit like fives. Ned was brilliant at it, he seemed to scoop the ball effortlessly from the air. Joey was pretty good too. Usually I keep up with anyone, but I was so set on outdoing Ned that I kept dropping the ball. Dickon just stood about smiling, looking pleased when Ned outdid himself. They plainly had a great relationship, more than most brothers.

In the bright light Dickon sometimes looked so thin and pale he was hardly there. Poor kid, I thought, and muffed my catch again.

"You're not very good at this, are you?" asked Ned, with his superior smile. He hadn't taken to me either, I could see that. He and Joey got on together okay, which needled me more. I was wishing that the Governor's wife would come and call them in when my sister's voice piped up behind us:

"Cwikey, Maisie's waving scweaming

mad! She's gone to the Chief Yeoman
or someone to post you missing. We've
all been told to look for you – ha*llo*!"
She'd caught sight of Ned, who was
looking flushed and triumphant in his
gear, keen-faced like a whippet.

Wadiant smile from Rilly.

Ned said, "Hi, there" cautiously.

"These are the Governor's kids – I

mean, his wards or something," I explained. "They live here. Rilly, I expect we'd better go."

She didn't listen. She took the ball from Ned's hand, bounced it against the wall, and caught it absentmindedly. After this bit of showing off, she said casually, "You could come back to tea with us, if you like. There's plenty of woom on the coach, no one will mind. School teas aren't bad, there's often waisin buns, and jam."

"I thought we would, anyway," said Ned loftily. (*Cheek.*) "It's pretty boring here in the evenings, with nothing to do but play jokes on the sentries. Dickon, would you like that?"

"Oh yes, *please*," said Dickon, eyes shining.

This was getting out of hand. Our Maisie wouldn't be in the mood for granting favours. I frowned at Rilly, who paid absolutely no attention.

"What sort of jokes?" she asked Ned eagerly.

"They're dead scared of the Tower, though they pretend not to be. We make funny noises behind them on dark nights. Their guns simply rattle in their hands. Dickon likes moaning in the chapel – or clanking about in the armour."

"And Ned makes splendid wailing noises where Anne Boleyn was put to death," added Dickon admiringly.

"I suppose they're simply scared of ghosts." Rilly looked scornful. *"I'm* not scared. They're not even interesting."

"Boleyn's certainly a bore," said Ned, as though he knew her personally. "Always complaining about her missing head. You'd think she'd be used to it by now."

"Shouldn't have lost it in the first place, should she?" said Dickon. "Joke, ha-ha." He turned a cartwheel on the grass.

All this talk of ghosts was making Joey shake again. He even looked thankful to see Dwight and Maisie approaching us under full steam.

"We're sorry, Miss Engleford. We got mixed up with another party," I said hastily before she could speak.

Her face went blotchy beetroot as though she might explode. "Michael Halliday, Joey M'basa, see the Headmaster after school."

"Aw, don't be hard on the kids, Maisie," said Dwight. "Weren't none of us over serious at their age. I bet you weren't, Brighteyes."

Brighteyes. I had to bite my lip to stop myself from grinning. Maisie thawed a bit, though she said severely, "Then we'll overlook it, this time. But they missed a lot, messing about out here. All that money wasted."

"We weren't just messing about," said Joey. "We met Ned and Dickon – the Governor's wards." He gave me a crafty wink, meaning, "She'll like that." You couldn't deny they were both what she'd call presentable.

"Oh yes?" she said vaguely, and looked straight through them. Rather

rude, I thought. Maybe she was still
upset and just holding back her fury
in the way people do, I've noticed, in
front of someone who fancies them.

"Could they come back with us for
tea?" put in Rilly, seizing her chance.
Maisie merely said "Oh?" again,
doubtfully, looking about her, and:
"The coach will be waiting. There's

no time to ask permission, dear, or go looking for anybody."

I didn't mind losing Ned, who was getting up my nose. But I felt sorry for Dickon, who looked dreadfully disappointed. I guess the thought of a raisin bun with jam had cheered him up after all that standing about, and being sickly.

"Come, anyway," Rilly whispered in Ned's ear. "She won't notice till it's too late."

"Of course. I always meant to," he said loftily. "It will do Dickon good to get out of this damp hole."

It was really boring that Ned had decided to tag along. I hoped Maisie would notice them and turf them off the coach – or at least that he and Dickon wouldn't linger over tea.

Chapter Three

WE WERE SOON hustling along not
to keep the coach waiting. I glanced
back once towards the Tower to see if
the others were keeping up. All I
could see through dazzling sunshine
was Joey and Rilly behind us, both
talking eagerly while paying no
attention to each other. Maybe Ned
and Dickon had slipped off
somewhere, after all. Then the sun
went in and there they were again,
just behind Joey. A trick of the light.

Dwight and Maisie checked us in on
to the coach: taking no chances, not
after the way Joey and I had lost

ourselves. We sat down in the second-best seats – the front ones were for the teachers. Rilly's closest friend, a hunky redhaired girl called Bella, had latched on to her, rather to Rilly's annoyance. She was waiting for Ned, I guessed, but Bella dragged her to the back of the coach, their usual place.

Ned and Dickon slipped on amongst

the rest. They sat down in the
teachers' seats. I was waiting for
Maisie to turn them off, but she was
waving little Tommy Twite on board.
  Ned was settling Dickon into the
window seat so that he could see out
properly. I tapped him on the
shoulder. "Hey! You can't sit there –
it's the teachers' place."

"Dickon likes it. You do let your tutors boss you around, don't you? I wouldn't stand for it."

Ned's smile had that curl of the lip that was so annoying.

We'll see about that, I thought, waiting expectantly for Maisie's reaction. It would be goodbye to Ned – though a shame for Dickon, who was looking flushed and excited.

"We've never been on one of these before," he told me. "I always wanted to, but we knew no one who could take us." The Governor must be pretty mean not to give a sick kid a simple treat like that.

Maisie was saying, "Hurry up, Amy, dear, don't hang about." The last one of us was shooed on board.

Dwight and Maisie followed. I held my breath, waiting to see insufferable Ned squashed flat. And to my utter disbelief, that's exactly what happened! Dwight and Maisie sat down on them as if they *weren't there*.

For a moment I couldn't believe my eyes. Thought I'd had sunstroke, or something. Beside me Joey went "Whhhhhhhheeeeeeeee!" like a deflating balloon.

Maisie looked round to ask, "Did you speak, dear?"

She was by the window and seemed to have simply absorbed Dickon – I could just see the top of his head sticking out above her shoulder. Burly Dwight had done even worse by Ned, who had vanished completely – except for one foot visible in the gangway.

I didn't have to look at Joey to know

what he was feeling. He was making
crowing noises now, like somebody
with whooping cough.

Dwight turned round. "Say, Maisie,
what's with the kid? He's choking."

"Driver, don't start!" Maisie
commanded. "Get up, Michael, let me
see to Joey. Has he been eating
sweets?"

They hauled poor Joey out into the

gangway, where they laid him flat and began practising first aid, in a confused sort of way. Holding Joey upside-down made him worse. Then Dwight pumped at his chest while Maisie tried blowing in his mouth. One girl cried, "Loosen his collar!" which didn't help since he was wearing a T-shirt. In between treatment he gave strangled cries.

I wasn't feeling too good myself, but it seemed the wrong moment to say so, specially in front of Ned. He had reappeared alongside Dickon immediately the teachers stood up. The brothers must have hung around the tourists for ages, I realised, waiting for somebody like Joey who could see them.

"I suppose Richard the Third was your murderous uncle and you're the Princes," I said at last. I thought myself pretty smart to manage that, when I was literally shaking in my shoes.

"Yes, he was, the beast," said Ned resentfully.

"Oh, poor Uncle Dickie!" mourned Dickon. "Everyone's horrid about him. He couldn't help it that we got those *smothering* chest colds in the Bloody Tower. He didn't let on for

months, and then of course they thought he'd done us in."

Ned patted his shoulder. His smile looked rather cynical, I thought. "Cheer up, young 'un – old Crookback got the Throne, anyway."

Just then Joey caught sight of them again. He yelped.

"Look here, you two, Joey's had enough," I said indignantly. "You jolly

well get off this coach! Let him alone."

"Michael, how dare you speak to us like that?" exclaimed Maisie, but she was luckily distracted when Joey suddenly leaped up and took a running jump from the coach.

"Heck!" said Ned (he must have been listening to Dwight). "Can't he make up his mind? Come on, Dickon," and he went loping after Joey, going clean through Maisie in his stride.

I followed. Not that I wouldn't be glad to see the last of the two Princes, but I had to stick by Joey. He was standing on the Hill, taking deep breaths and rolling his eyes. When he saw Ned and Dickon coming he bolted again. Maisie and Dwight tumbled out after us, with Dwight yelling "Stop that kid!" to a St John

ambulance man coming in the
opposite direction.

Between them they hustled Joey into
a first aid post. I heard them
muttering about "too much heat," and
offering Joey water. There was a loud
gulping sound.

Ned and Dickon were waiting

outside with me, like two spaniels. In the bright light they looked just like two ordinary boys, though smarter than most.

"Please go home, *please*," I begged them. "You're scaring him silly. He's allergic to – to you."

Ned kicked moodily at a pebble. "No," he said at last. "Absolutely not. He'll just have to get used to us. There aren't very many like him these days, we've been waiting for so long. We escaped last century for a bit with a woman who spent all day with crystal balls. *She* was chuffed to have us, but *we* couldn't take it." He shuddered, like me. "The company! Her American Indian Chieftain was a class act, but when she shifted to the Cromwells we went home."

"Ned says we must have standards," explained Dickon. "Quite a few people in the Tower are okay even if they're dull."

I was almost in despair. "How long exactly do you mean to stay? Joey's home is quite ordinary, not exciting."

Ned shrugged. "Well, it's not too thrilling when most of the people you're shut up with after dark have lost their heads. We've had five hundred years of them."

"There's one nice Centurion who tells good stories about the Roman Legions," put in Dickon. "He got drowned by an Ancient Briton."

"*And* there's lovely Queen Jane Grey, isn't there, young'un?" said Ned, with a quirky look.

Dickon blushed. "You're not to tease," he said. "She's not there often, anyway."

By now my quiver had almost stopped. They sounded so – so everyday, that I was beginning to

get used to them. But I was pretty sure Joey wouldn't. And I'd begun to suspect Ned had no intention of ever going back.

"Joey won't like it," I said.

Just then Maisie put her head out of the First Aid Post. "Is that you, Michael? Why are you talking to yourself? Come inside a moment, dear."

I went, muttering to Ned, "Stay out there, or I'll kill you." A pretty odd threat, when you think of it. I heard him laugh.

Joey was sitting on a chair, looking a little better. "Are they still there?" he mouthed.

I nodded. "They're okay. They're quite ordinary, really," I whispered. That was a daft thing to say, too. They never had been ordinary to start with, and they were less ordinary now.

"Joey says he felt dizzy. The heat, I

expect," Maisie told me. "He can lie down at the back of the coach. Will you sit with him? Your sister and Bella must move forward."

"That's a great idea," I said. "Come on, Joey." I took him by the arm, praying he wouldn't bolt again outside. I murmured in his ear, "We'll give them a jolly good tea, then get rid of them." (I couldn't imagine how, but one thing at a time, as my mum says.)

I felt him flinch, and hissed, "Show some bottle, mate! Where's the M'basa fighting style?" I was pretty amazed at my own, but seeing Joey so down had somehow strengthened me. We've been best buddies since primary.

There was no sign of the brothers outside. My spirits rose, till I caught sight of Dickon sitting crosslegged on the bonnet of a super jet-black Rolls Royce, all gleam and glitz. Ned was inside it, fiddling with the gears. It was starting to move . . .

"Ned – stop it!" I yelled. "*Brake!*" People turned to stare at me, then at the car. A short stout bloke nearby let out a heartfelt screech and began to run towards it, waving his arms.

Like a splendid ship in full sail the Roller moved out into the road, coasting downhill under its own

steam. Somehow Ned was outside it, standing on the kerb, watching his work with an aloof expression. Dickon jumped off the bonnet, laughing. Several people began to chase the car. There was an awful grinding sound as it mounted the pavement and came to rest against a traffic sign. Its owner was wringing his hands.

"Wow!" exclaimed Joey, forgetting his own worries. "There goes a

£20,000 repair job!" (His dad owns a garage, so he has an eye for these things.)

A crowd had gathered round the Roller, a policeman too. Someone was saying, "Stupid idiot must have left the brake off."

"I braked *firmly*," the owner was sobbing. "I'll swear it."

The cop scratched his head, disbelievingly. "A lot of damage you've done, sir." He took out his notebook, and began to write.

Joey was admiring the Roller.

"Push off," glowered its owner. The cop looked at Joey curiously.

"Know anything about this, son?" he asked.

"I was *miles* away." Joey retreated in a dignified way, only to find himself confronting Ned. He went shuddery again. "It was *you*!"

"I only touched things here and there . . . Nice cars, aren't they? Not like horses, though. I had a charger called Roland. Dickon had a pony." Ned sighed. "We don't have them any more, they've moved on."

Joey edged away, eyeing him sideways. Good that he wasn't panicking, at least. After all, he'd got on pretty well with Ned at first, almost made me jealous. I began to feel hopeful we'd get out of this all right, somehow. Get them on the coach, give them a nice tea, then perhaps we could persuade them to go home.

Chapter Four

IT WAS ALMOST five o'clock when the coach pulled up outside our school. Maisie had insisted on Joey lying down. I sat by his feet while Ned and Dickon crammed in together by the other window. It was a bit of a squash – at least, it would have been if I'd dared stick my left elbow out. No, thanks: I was careful to keep away from them. Cold shivers were running up and down my spine again.

"Sit on me if you like," said Ned, with an obliging grin. "I won't mind." He knew jolly well that *I* would.

Dickon enjoyed the journey, anyway.

"Oh look!" he kept saying "Look at *that*. Is it a bus? Shall we all go to the cinema, Mike? We never see a film, not even on telly."

"The Governor's got one, but his wife watches dreary programmes," sighed Ned. "We switch over, and she just switches back. She thought it was the TV people's fault. She rowed them no end."

"How come you speak just like us?" I asked.

"'Haste thee from my sight, varlet!' Is that what you'd expect? Not after five hundred years mucking round the bleeding place, mate!" Ned sounded bitter.

"Couldn't you move on, like your horses?" I asked hopefully.

"How funny, that's what Queen Jane says!" exclaimed Dickon. "But we don't seem able to. Ned thinks it may

be something to do with Uncle Dickie, but he won't say what. Anyway, we couldn't shift and leave the poor old bloke alone."

"You mean to say he's still there?" gasped Joey.

"Yes – he seems to have something on his mind. We should have brought him along, he'd have liked an outing on a smashing coach."

Cor! I knew what Joey was thinking, because I was too. This Uncle Dickie would have been bad news, all right. We'd got lucky, in some ways.

"Is that a palace?" Dickon asked, as we drove up the Mall. "Is that a Royal Standard?"

"Those are Plantagenet leopards, all right, but they've quartered them," Ned said critically.

"They shouldn't fly it when you're not there," grumbled Dickon. "Cheek!

Usurpers!" That was going a bit far, but I held my tongue.

"Are they really who I think they are?" whispered Joey.

"Spot on, man," I said gloomily.

Rilly and Bella were sitting in our first seats. Now and then Rilly turned to look our way with a puzzled frown. No wadiant smiles for Ned.

It set me thinking. Couldn't she see him now? Was she too far off? And why did no one else see the Princes, apart from me and Joey? Maybe we'd been around Joey so long – specially me – that a slice of his gift or whatever it was had wiped off on us. He was always in and out of our house. That must be it. He was some sort of loony magnetic field. I was proud of my scientific deduction.

Then a nasty thought struck me. Suppose I'd become too Joey-positive!

The brothers might start coming
home with *me*. I'd do almost anything
to help poor Joey, but not quite that.

"You will think of something, won't
you, Mike?" he pleaded, as we got off
the coach. "Don't let me down."

"Of course," I assured him airily.
"Just leave it to uncle." A bad choice
of words, considering.

Maisie was advancing on us. "Joey, I
think you should go straight home. I'll

ask your mother to collect you."

"Oh, please don't, Miss Engleford! I'm quite all right now," protested Joey, horrified.

"Quite sure, dear?" She looked him over doubtfully. "You had quite a nasty turn on the coach."

"*Absolutely* sure. Besides, Mum was going out. She knew me and Mike were going to play football with friends." (First I'd heard of it.)

Maisie gave way quite easily. Her thoughts were all on Dwight, I could see that. "Very well, but try not to run about much, Joey." What a daft idea! How else do you play football?

Ned and Dickon were waiting impatiently for us.

"Hurry up," urged Dickon. "I'm famished. Where's this famous tea?"

Rilly suddenly appeared at my elbow. She'd shed Bella and was giving Ned the same come-on misty looks as Maisie was giving love-sick Dwight. "Sit by me," she cooed. "I'll get you loads of stwarbewwy jam."

Joey and I exchanged looks, both of us hoping she wouldn't yelp if someone sat down on them.

Luckily, not everyone was having tea that day, so there was plenty of room. With Ned and Dickon on each side of her and the jam dish before her Rilly was soon plying them with luscious sticky buns as fast as she could go.

"Amaryllis!" exclaimed the tea monitor's voice behind us, "You're a greedy pig. That's about the seventh bun you've grabbed, and half the jam. Leave some for the others."

"Ned's a guest. He's so hungry," explained Rilly.

"Oh yeah? You're too old to be playing the invisible playmate game!" snorted the monitor witheringly as she moved away.

"Funny thing to say," puzzled Rilly. Dickon choked on a last bite of bun. Ned grinned.

"Come on, let's go out and play football," said Joey hastily, catching my eye.

We haven't a proper playing field, just a rough patch of ground which the school owns, where other kids

sometimes come to play. It was nearly
six o'clock by now. Most people had
gone home, though Bella had
appeared as if from nowhere.

"I'm rather glad she hasn't taken to
Ned," Rilly whispered to me. "He
must have got across her – she looks
straight through him."

"Extraordinary," I said, and decided
we wouldn't play for long. Life seemed
to be full of pitfalls. That old Tower
brought no one any good. I still hadn't
thought of a solution, in spite of my
scientific brain.

Joey's a keen footballer. I mean,
other people might go to church on
Sundays, but he just gazes at
photographs of Gazza. However, even
Joey didn't seem that keen to play
now. He hates a game with girls
anyway. It's annoying when they're
weak and worse if they're strong like

Bella and shoulder everyone aside Gazza-style.

We kicked his new football about for a while. I was quite enjoying myself, except that when I was down the far end of the ground I'd look back and see only Joey and the girls, or sometimes Ned's or Dickon's feet. Then they'd be whole again, and one of Ned's stupendous kicks would send the ball flashing down the field. Sometimes it seemed to take off by itself.

"Mike!" whispered Rilly urgently, "dweadful funny things keep happening to my eyes . . . sometimes Ned absolutely *vanishes*. Bella seems to think there's only Joey!" She rubbed her eyes and blinked furiously.

"Some weird bug going round," I told her quickly. "Look how oddly Joey was acting on the coach. If you and Bella are having funny vision you'd better go home with her. Lie down before it comes on badly. *Joey!*" I yelled across the ground, "Time to go!"

I was counting on Bella bullying Rilly. And she did, dragging her away in spite of Rilly protesting she wanted to come with us.

"You can't," I said firmly. I didn't want her catching on and blabbing about it everywhere. People get hooked on publicity, don't they? If Ned once got his story in the newspapers he might get such a taste for it he'd never go. It would be worse than all those books on Lady Di. I shuddered to think of it, more than I'd shuddered on the coach.

"I'll be seeing you at Mike's one of these days," promised Ned, with a teasing smile.

"Weally, twuly?" sighed my sister.
"Bye, Ned. Bye, Dickon."

Bella looked disturbed.

I said hurriedly, "Don't worry, Bella, it's the heat. Rilly, you go with Bella and watch her videos." I seized Joey by the arm to walk him quickly away. Ned and Dickon followed.

Now, you may think I'm brilliant, with a great future before me, and I'd not say you're wrong. Because it was on that walk to Joey's place, with Joey beginning to wilt again now he'd had more time to see what he was lumbered with, that I formed my Plan. Lateral thinking, they call it: I saw the whole thing from another angle. It was useless appealing to Ned. We must counter attack instead.

"You'll stay overnight, won't you, Mike?" Joey begged, as we reached his door. The whites of his eyes were rolling again. He has a two-tier bunk in his bedroom and I guessed he was visualizing the brothers in the top half. "You can share my bunk," he said, "if –"

" – it's necessary," I finished for him.

Dickon was looking rather tired after the football. He sniffed a bit dolefully. "I shall miss Queen Jane – she isn't stuck over here like us, but she comes back to tuck me up in bed." His voice trembled. Ned put an arm round him protectively.

I was liking him for that when he spoilt it by saying, "Is this your hovel? It's not as large as the mews where I kept my hawks, before we went to the Tower."

Hovel! The Tower was far more suitable for the brothers, I decided, and I determined to put my brilliant Plan into action as soon as possible.

Chapter Five

LUCKILY, JOEY'S MUM was still out, and Joey knew just where to find the front door key. As we let ourselves in we could hear the voices of his younger brothers playing next door.

"What a dear little room!" cried Dickon, running ahead into the cluttered living room. "Brill! You've got a super telly. The Governor's wife never watches *Neighbours*. If we put it on she says, "Bother, another fault", and rings to complain."

"It won't be on now, you clot! Anyway, I'd rather have sport," said Ned, wresting the zapper from him.

They had a brotherly tussle on the sofa.

Joey was reading a note: "Mum says she and Dad will both be late. There's cold food in the fridge, or go next door."

"Good news," I said. "Come on, let's get supper going." And I told Ned, "There's sport on Sky, I bet. You can watch, while Joey and I rustle up some sandwiches."

"See well to it, varlets," said Ned, with a wave of his hand and a wicked look at me. "Bring us small ale too, or you shall be whipped with invisible thongs." He'd got possession of the zapper, Dickon pinned down with one elbow, and his muddy feet on Joey's mother's favourite chair.

I hustled Joey into the kitchen. He was looking jittery again.

"Think he meant it?" he muttered.

"He was just teasing," I said stoutly, not quite sure. "Listen, I've made a Plan. Just go along with anything I suggest when we go up to bed, okay?" I wouldn't tell him more. He might jib unless I rushed him into it.

"You mean, you can *really* get rid of them?" he asked. "Keep my new football, if you do." I could see he didn't put much trust in me.

"I'm *almost* sure," I said cautiously.

"I couldn't bear it if they start coming through shut doors," he said, quivering.

Neither could I. "Keep your cool – you deal with the ham sandwiches while I find some ginger beer," I told him.

Joey began to dither, but I was already opening a can. We made them a super supper. A farewell feast, I assured myself. When we staggered in with the tray Ned cast an approving eye over it. He zapped off the sports channel.

"Just in time, varlets. Dickon's feeling weepy."

"I don't want to go back, truly,"
moaned Dickon. "It's just that Queen
Jane will be missing me, I'm sure she
will. I'll miss her too . . . and her
stories of Over There. Can't we go
back for just an hour, Ned?"

"You can, if you like. I'm staying,"
said Ned briskly. "Get some food
inside you, you'll feel better. Anyway,
you won't miss old Salisbury cackling
away for the thousandth time about
how they chased her round the block."

He took a gulp of ginger beer. "I say, this is something else again. Pour some for Dickon."

We'd almost finished when we heard Joey's mother coming in, muttering grimly to herself, and sounding mad as fire after her long evening stint at a superstore checkout. Then she appeared in the doorway like a thundercloud, mopping her forehead with one of Mr M'basa's red and white handkerchiefs.

"Oh my, son," she moaned, "sure is

the hottest night." She plumped down on the sofa. She's a large woman, so both Ned and Dickon vanished, except for one of Ned's hands holding a glass of ginger beer. "Right handy of you, Joey – you good to your old ma," she sighed, and took the glass without looking where it came from. Three thirsty gulps and the beer was gone.

"My drink!" said Ned, outraged.

Mrs M'basa looked round her, puzzled. "Someone say sumpin'?" Seemed she had a spot of Joey-ness about her.

"My drink!" shouted Ned again. Out came his other arm sideways from her wobbly bosom and slapped a sandwich in her face.

Wow! Was there trouble! Up she

jumped like a kangaroo, spluttering and wiping mixed peanut and coleslaw from her eyes, seized hold of Joey and shook him mightily. "How come you do saucy thing like that, boy! Jus' wait till you Dad come home! Bed now, this minute!"

She raised a hefty hand, and Joey left the room rocket-wise before she could take in the extra beer mugs. Dickon trotted after him nervously, followed by Ned wearing his wicked grin. He moved fast-ish, though, I noticed.

Mrs M'basa flumped back on the sofa with a shaky groan. "I goin' crazy, Mike lad. Jus' thought I seen sumpin' go out that door –"

"A funny bug's going round – Joey, me and Rilly, we've all been seeing things," I told her. "Joey's asked me to stay tonight. Shall I wash up?" I

headed for the door with the tray
before she could take a good look at it.

When I went upstairs two sponges
were weaving around, floating
between invisible hands. I reached the
top step, and saw Ned and Dickon
juggling with them outside Joey's
room. The door was open. Joey was
sitting gloomily on the side of his
bunk. Downhearted.

"We're sleeping in with Joey," called Dickon excitedly.

It was the moment for my Plan.

"Bit stuffy for us all," I objected. "There's a fine big bed in the spare room upstairs. Let's creep up now and show them, Joey."

I thought he was going to faint or hit me. "Man, you gone mad, or sumpin'?" he muttered.

I pinched his arm menacingly. "Remember what I told you? Come *on*."

I led the way, Joey hanging back.

Ned inspected the room critically. It had an enormous brass bedstead, and heavy curtains. "Not bad . . . we'll make do with this, Dickon. Ho, varlet, fetch clean linen."

"Okay, Your Highness" I said. "Try it for trampolining first. It's great for bouncing on."

"No, Mike, no," cried Joey. "You're not to, Ned."

"Not to?" said Ned, raising a princely eyebrow. "*Me?*"

He leapt on to the bed in his muddy boots and began to jump, higher and higher.

Then –

Well, it was like a whirlwind, or the Chunnel Shuttle with its lights on. Something twice as big as Mrs M'basa, with glowing eyes, came through the closed door with a screech to shake the roof.

"Auntie Zeta!" moaned Joey.

"You Plantagenet white trash!" yelled his Auntie, foaming at the mouth. "How come you think youself fit fer leapin' on m'bed? How come you dare terrorize m' li'l Joey M'basa, you runt? You gettin' such a hidin' as you Uncle never dream of. I'll

Plantagenet you!" She seized Ned by the scruff, threw him over her knee, and laid into him with a handy curtain cord.

What a scene. Joey and me clutching one another. Dickon sobbing, "Jane, Jane. I want Queen Jane." And Ned letting go of princeliness to bawl at the top of his lungs as Auntie Zeta goes whang, whang, whang with the curtain cord in her ample fist.

At last Ned managed to wriggle free and hurtle Shuttle-wise for the door, with Auntie Zeta in pursuit, grinding her teeth and shouting, "You don't come back here no more, boy! I comin' home to tell you Uncle Richard on you."

Dickon seemed reluctant to follow them. Then luckily – *did* I imagine it? – a misty girlish person with a small gap between her chin and shoulders floated in to seize him in her arms and bear him off in Auntie Zeta's wake.

"Mike, you're *the* most brilliant person I ever met in all my life," cried Joey, beaming all over his face.

"Thanks," I said modestly. After all,

we people with first-rate scientific brains hardly need telling so. "Can I truly have your football?"

That wasn't quite the end, though. A few days later Joey told me he was daydreaming about the Harlem Globetrotters in class, when Auntie Zeta's voice came through strongly, like on the telephone:

"Ain't comin' home again, Joey M'basa. Go sleep soundly in m'bed, child. This Tower needin' me: young Jane mean well, but she spoil they children rotten. Ned, he learnin' manners now. L'il Dickon havin' goosefat chest rub, an' their Uncle Dickie gettin' flannel drawers – a gennelman like he can catch sumpin' mighty awkward on a draughty staircase . . ." Joey said she faded out then. Bad connection, he supposed.

That was the last he ever heard of

her. Mind you, the old Tower itself hit the headlines soon afterwards, when a large black lady was seen about the place after sunset, polishing the headsman's block or dusting down the armour. The number of visitors doubled, several sentries deserted, and there was one accident. "Midnight, it were, and it come an' give me cocoa, din't it?" explained Sergeant Blethers, Victim. "Lunnon Ospital they takes me to, fer shock." He was on TV.

"Sounds like my Auntie Zeta all right," said Joey proudly. "Ghosts can be quite protective, can't they? Look at Queen Jane."

We never saw the Plantagenets again – I mean, Joey and I together didn't. Years later, my form went to a concert in the Tower. Mind, I had reservations, but I felt there was little risk, as Joey wasn't coming too.

There was no sign of Ned or Dickon at first. Then, as we were leaving, I

had a hazy sighting of them getting on a Spanish tourist coach. They must have found someone else like Joey. A feudal-looking thug, one shoulder all askew, was holding Dickon's hand – their physically-challenged Uncle Dickie, I suppose. At least we'd been spared *him*.

I wonder if Auntie Zeta knew they had escaped? Poor Plantagenets – they were casting nervous looks behind them. That was how Dickon caught sight of me. He waved and smiled delightedly. I didn't wave back, I'm afraid, in case he took it for encouragement. But I did hope he'd have an absolutely super time in Barcelona, getting well and strong again after all those years of jumping out at sentries from the Bloody Tower.

As for my friend Joey M'basa, he no longer has a fear of ghosts.

"Man, if I get stuck with someone else," he says, "I'll nip down to the Tower on a bus an whistle up m' Auntie. Why, think of it, Mike, the M'basa family is the only one in Britain to have given the old place a bigger draw than all the Queen's ancestors together."

These days he sleeps upstairs and sound as a dormouse in Auntie Zeta's bed.